For my girl Maddy —
stretch for the starlight.

Quarto is the authority on a wide range of topics.

Quarto educates, entertains and enriches the lives of
our readers—enthusiasts and lovers of hands-on living.
www.quartoknows.com

First published in Great Britain in 2003 by Frances Lincoln Children's
Books, The Old Brewery, 6 Blundell Street, London N7 9BH
www.franceslincoln.com

First paperback edition published in Great Britain in 2007
This paperback edition published in Great Britain in 2016

A catalogue record for this book is available from the British Library.

ISBN 978-1-84780-813-4

Set in Bembo Semi-Bold
Designed by Sarah Massini

Printed in China

9 8 7 6 5 4 3

Visit the Anholt website at www.anholt.co.uk

PHOTOGRAPHIC ACKNOWLEDGEMENTS
Please note, the pages in this book are not numbered.
The story begins on page 6.

Paintings by Claude Monet (1840-1926):

Front cover (detail) & Page 15 right: *The Japanese Bridge,*
1895. Photo © Christie's Images.

Page 13: *The Rose Path at Giverny*, 1920-22 (detail),
Musée Marmottan Monet, Paris, France/Bridgeman Images.

Page 14 left: *Nympheas et Agapanthes (Waterlillies a.*
Agapanthus), 1914-17, Musée d'Orsay, Paris, akg-images.

Page 14 right: Grainstacks at the end of the Summer. Monet,
Claude (1840-1926) Credit: Musée d'Orsay, Paris, France/
Bridgeman Images.

Page 15 left: *The Poplars*, 1881 (oil on canvas), Monet,
Claude (1840-1926) / Private Collection / Photo ©
Christie's Images / Bridgeman Images.

Pages 18-19 (outside): *Two Weeping Willows*, 1914-18
(details of left and right section). Musée de l'Orangerie, Paris,
France/Bridgeman Images.

Pages 18-19 (inside): *Waterlilies: Morning,* 1914-18
(details of left and centre left section). Musée de l'Orangerie,
Paris, France/Bridgeman Images.

Page 30: *Portrait of Claude Monet at Giverny, c.*1913. Guitry,
Sacha (1885-1957). Musée Marmottan Monet, Paris, France/
Bridgeman Images.

The Magical Garden of
Claude Monet

LAURENCE ANHOLT

Frances Lincoln
Children's Books

"I wish we had a garden," said Julie.

She looked down at the grey river, which ran through the city.
Even Louey the greyhound was bored of being inside.

"As soon as I have finished this painting," said Julie's mother,
"I'll take you on a journey to the most wonderful garden in the world.
It belongs to my old friend, the painter, Claude Monet."

They took a big black train beside the twisting river,

far out of the city ...

... and into the countryside.

Then Louey began to run,

down the hill and into a lane

where a huge wall stood

around a mysterious garden.

"Stop Louey!" called Julie, but
it was too late - Louey had gone!

Julie didn't know what to do.
She got down on her hands and
knees and wriggled inside.

It was like crawling into
a dreamy world, where twisting
plants grew tall as trees.

Julie ran around a corner
and almost knocked over
a big man with a spade.

The man had a straw hat
and a huge white beard.

"Oh!" said Julie, "I am looking
for my dog. Are you the gardener?"

"I suppose I am," said the man.
"Come and look.

"One day, these tiny seedlings will grow into big flowers. But a gardener has to be very patient... just like a painter."

Then Julie realised - "You are Claude Monet!" she gasped.

"Yes," laughed the old man, "I am Claude Monet!"

Together they searched for Louey – along the shady path, deeper and deeper into the magical garden, until it seemed as if they had left the real world behind.

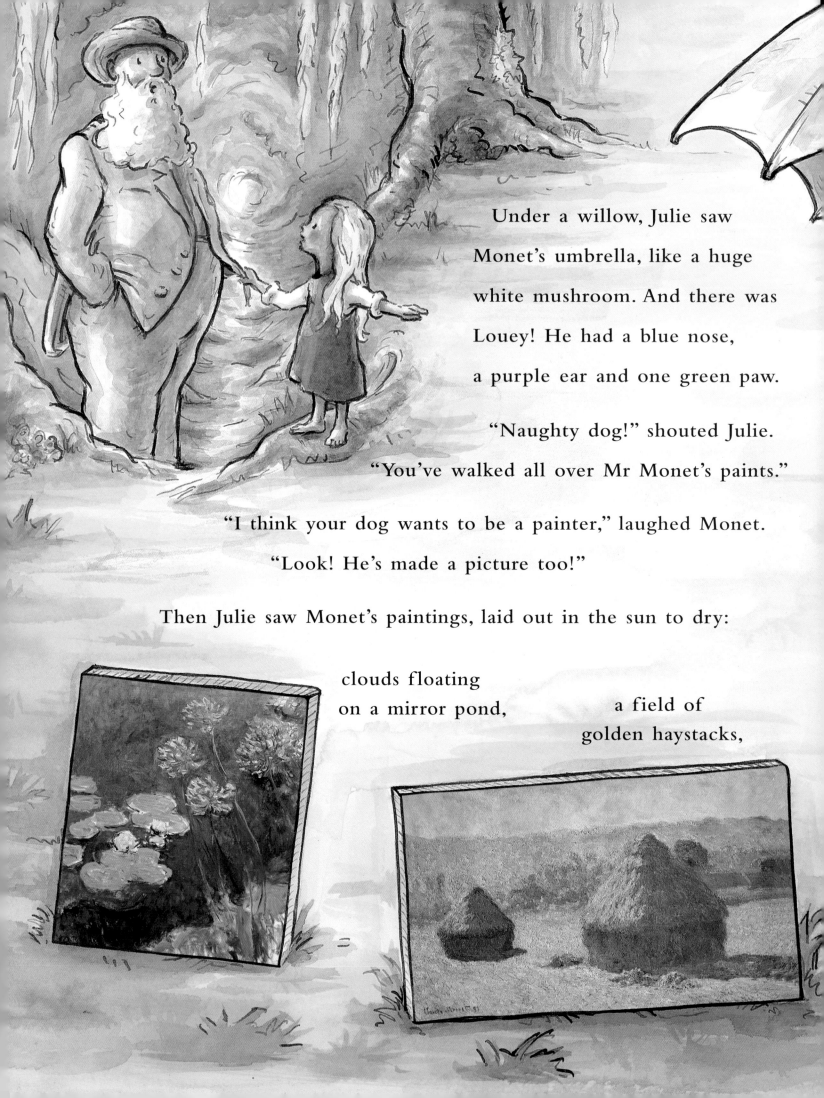

Under a willow, Julie saw
Monet's umbrella, like a huge
white mushroom. And there was
Louey! He had a blue nose,
a purple ear and one green paw.

"Naughty dog!" shouted Julie.
"You've walked all over Mr Monet's paints."

"I think your dog wants to be a painter," laughed Monet.

"Look! He's made a picture too!"

Then Julie saw Monet's paintings, laid out in the sun to dry:

clouds floating
on a mirror pond,

a field of
golden haystacks,

a little
Japanese
bridge.

a row
of wispy
poplars,

The brush marks glowed like flowers in a garden.

They turned the handle on a
rickety gate and stepped inside.

It was like a garden *inside*
a garden — a wild, wet watery
garden, where willows bowed
over a silent pool.

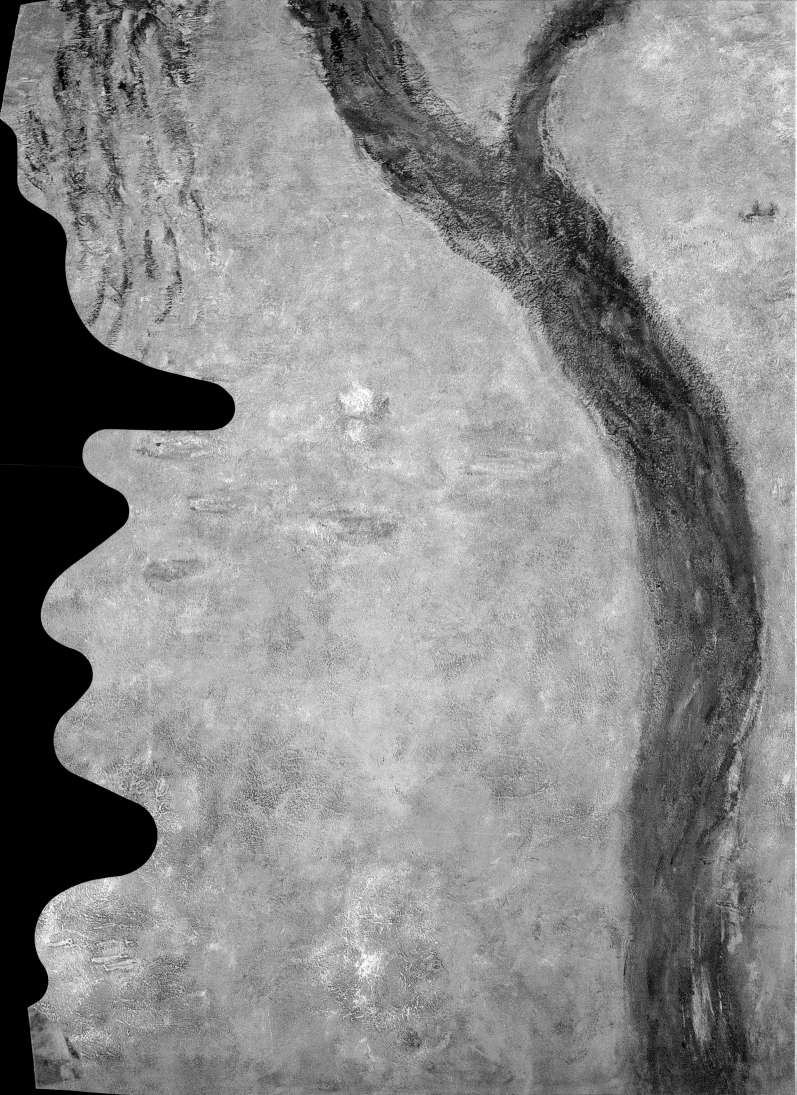

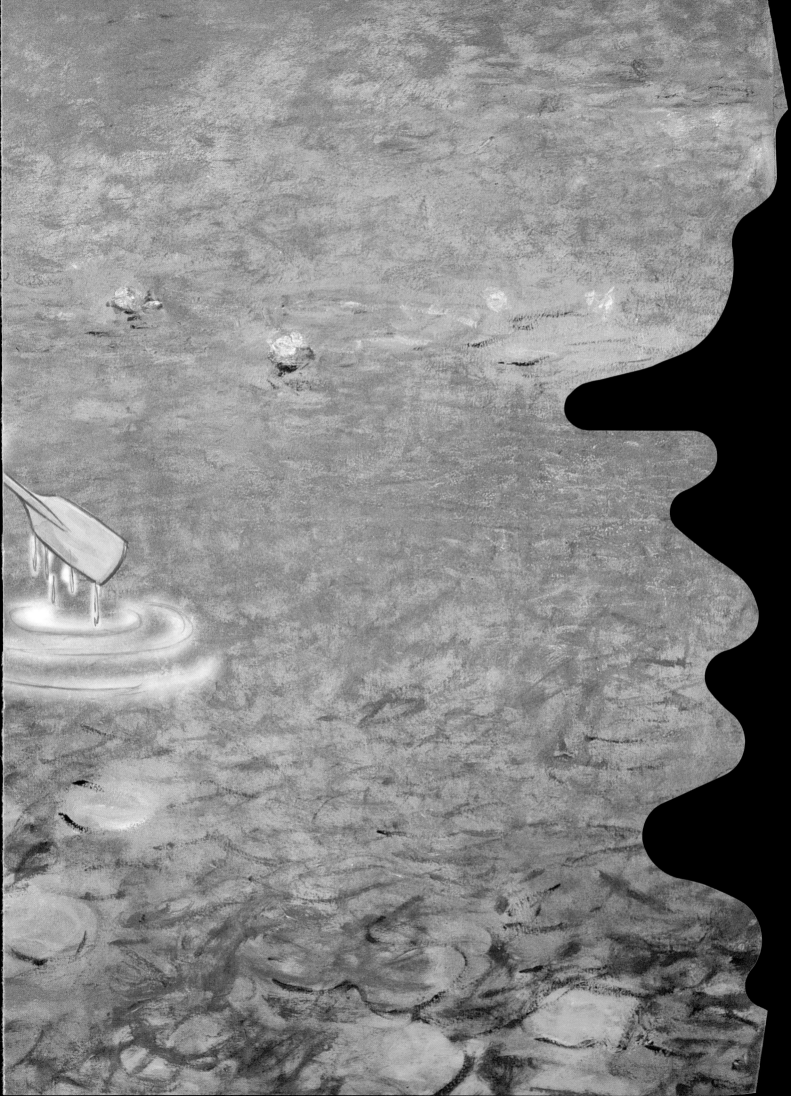

Together they crossed
the green bridge.

When they rowed across the pond,

it felt like floating

in Mr Monet's paintings.

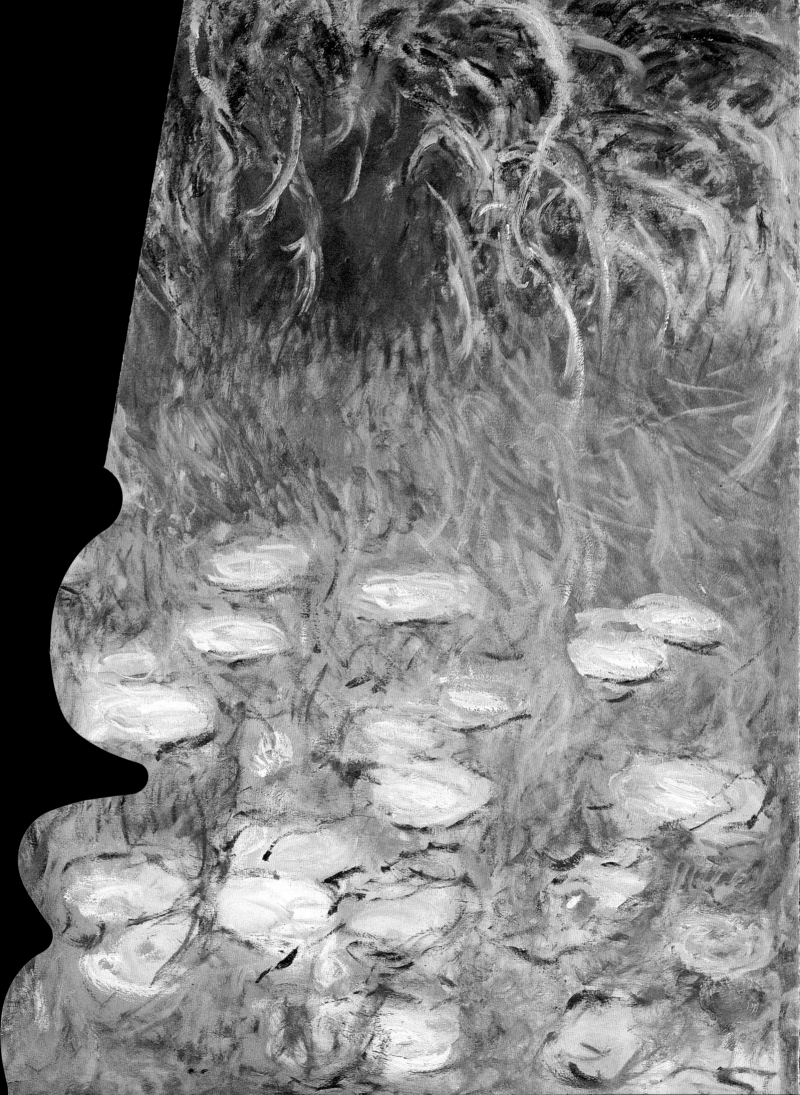

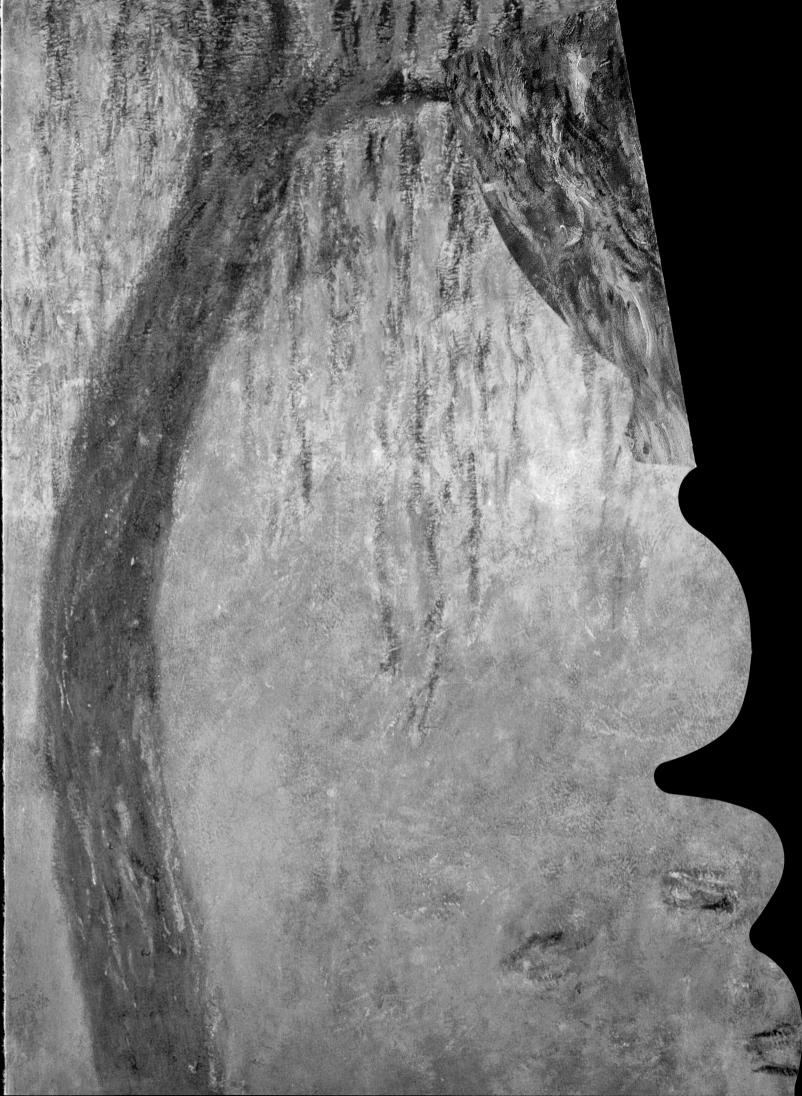

Julie heard the splash of the oars and birds calling in the trees.

All around them, lilies sparkled like a midnight sky. When they reached the very middle of the pool, Monet stretched into the dark water and pulled out one flower - the biggest lily of all, as bright as a silver star.

"A little present from my water-garden," he said.

They walked back towards the house and Monet pushed open a huge studio door.

"Here is my biggest idea of all," he said proudly. "I am trying to paint the most enormous water garden in the world. When you stand in the middle, you will feel as if you have dived into a pool."

"It will be amazing!" said Julie.

For a moment, Monet looked sad. "But to tell the truth, I wonder if I will ever finish," he said. "I'm old now and my eyesight is bad."

Julie thought for a moment. "You will need to be very patient," she said, "like a gardener."

"Yes," he smiled. "Just like a gardener."

Then Claude Monet pulled out a big watch. "Four o'clock precisely," he said. "Time for tea."

Waiting in the yellow dining-room, surrounded by pictures from Japan, sat Mrs Monet and Julie's mother.

"Here are your little runaways!" said Monet.

Then it was time to leave.
Monet walked with them as far as the river.

Louey wanted to say goodbye too, but as
he jumped up, Julie's beautiful lily went
flying into the river.

"Oh Louey!" shouted Julie.
"That was a special lily!"

They took the train back
to the city, and even Louey
was tired. The garden seemed
like a distant dream.

But in the middle of the night, Julie heard Louey whining
to go outside. She tiptoed through the apartment.
Beneath the balcony, something was sparkling on the river.

Julie ran outside, and stretched into the dark water.
She pulled out a lily – as bright as a silver star.

"Perhaps it's a little present from the water garden," she whispered.

And as the city slept, she breathed in the sweet smell of the magical garden of Claude Monet.

Born in 1840, Claude Monet lived all his life along the River Seine. He always preferred to paint outdoors and is often described as the father of Impressionism. Second only to his passion for painting was his love of Nature and gardening; he once paid a woodcutter to spare a row of trees he was painting.

In 1883, while still very poor, Monet rented the green and pink house at Giverny which became a beautiful home for his extended family. Over the years his fame increased and he became very rich indeed, eventually buying his house and employing gardeners to help create the water gardens – the subject of much of his later work.

Monet was immensely disciplined, usually rising at 4 a.m. and always insisting that the house ran like clockwork. He set equally high standards for his work: on one occasion a gardener was ordered to burn several paintings which Monet considered unsuccessful; on another, Monet threw his canvas, easel and brushes into the water!

During the First World War, fighting went on so near Monet's house that he could hear the guns, but although his son was killed in action, Monet refused to leave his beloved garden.

Monet had numerous young visitors at Giverny, but Julie is based on one very special girl – Julie Manet, daughter of the great Impressionist Berthe Morisot. Julie's mother and Monet were great friends and he owned several of Berthe's paintings. By coincidence, Julie was born on Monet's birthday. Julie's uncle was the painter Edouard Manet and many of the great artists and writers of the time were visitors to the apartment. Julie's greyhound Laertes (or 'Louey') was a gift from Renoir, who also presented her with a set of crayons (a novelty in those days), which helped to set Julie on the path to self-expression.

You can still visit the magical garden of Claude Monet – just one hour by train along the river from Paris. Visitors will see the yellow dining-room and the huge studio that the 76-year-old artist built for his last great masterpiece, the circular water lily series. You can wander along the path and over the Japanese bridge, just like Julie. Look down at the sparkling water and you'll see the lilies, as bright as silver stars.

MORE BOOKS IN THE ANHOLT'S ARTISTS SERIES

For over 20 years, the Anholt's Artists series has introduced readers to some of the world's most famous artists through the real children who knew them. Telling inspirational true stories and featuring reproductions of the artists' work, these titles bring art to life for children everywhere.

Anholt's Artists Activity Book
978-1-84507-911-6

Camille and the Sunflowers
978-0-71122-156-7

Cézanne and the Apple Boy
978-1-84780-604-8

Degas and the Little Dancer
978-0-71122-157-4

Leonardo and the Flying Boy
978-1-84780-816-5

Matisse, King of Colour
978-1-84780-043-5

Picasso and the Girl with a Ponytail
978-0-71121-177-3

Tell Us a Story, Papa Chagall
978-1-84780-339-9

"A great introduction to art . . . highly recommended."
– *The Observer*

Frances Lincoln titles are available from all good bookshops.
You can also buy books and find out more about your favourite titles,
authors and illustrators on our website: www.franceslincoln.com